MOG IN THE FOG

for Tom

MOG in the FOG

by Helen Nicoll
and Jan Pieńkowski

PUFFIN BOOKS

Goodbye Owl

Why won't you come?

Are we nearly there?

Mog wanted to climb the

highest mountain in the world

BONG

A Sherpa saw them land

Hello
I'm Tsing
This is Yak

I'm Meg
This is Mog

Yak

Meeow

Will you take us to the top?

O.K. I lead caravan

Oh dear oh dear

Very old bridge

CREAK

They crossed

many torrents

Up and up and up and up they climbed

It started to snow

Tsing took them to a cave

Now we make tea

Good tea! Good butter in it

Yuk!

?

The sun came out. It was dazzling

What big feet!

Mog found some footprints

Mog! Mog! Where are you?

A huge cloud came down

sniff sniff

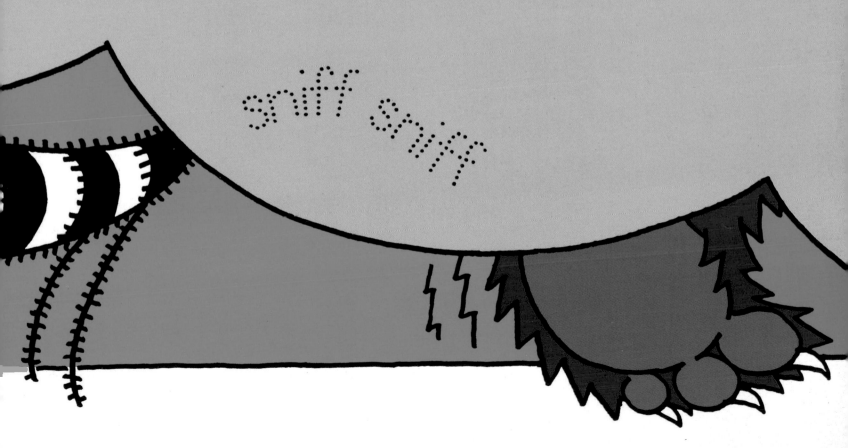

They were lost in the fog

Stay where you are!

I must just find Mog

Mog! Mog!

Is that you?

Sorry

YAK!

BUMP

Iceaxe, compass
Goggles and log
Help me, show me
Lead me to Mog

Oh! here you are

Meg made a spell

The fog started to lift

EEEK!!!

All the fog rolled away

Yeti!

Yak?

Meeow!

They all ran

and
did
not
stop
until
the
top

Yak

Mind how you go

Thanks!

Cheers!

They flew home

It was tea time

Pass the butter

Goodbye!